The Black Bag

The Black Bag

Roderick Rightt

Library of Congress Control Number: 2011917343

ISBN:	Hardcover	978-1-4653-7037-2
	Softcover	978-1-4653-7036-5
	eBook	978-1-4653-7038-9

Print information available on the last page.

Rev. date: 12/19/2019

To order additional copies of this book, contact:
Xlibris
1-888-795-4274
www.Xlibris.com
Orders@Xlibris.com
536450

Dedication

I want to first give thanks to our Lord and Savior Jesus Christ. Through him all things are possible.

I want to dedicate my first project to the strongest black woman I know, my mother. "Kristi D. Palmer"

I just want you to know that I love you and everything I've done, I do and will accomplish in the future I do so you can be proud when you say

"That's my son. I raised a boy into that man".

"Life hits hard,but it's meant to push you forward rather than knock you down"

-Roderick Rightt...

"I seen this vision while I was sitting in jail, and I tried my best to bring it to life. Welcome to my thoughts"

...Alday!

The Black bag is about this young guy named Percy known as P. He grew up in a foster home and on release he met a young lady named Fran that he calls snowflake. P has this mentality that he's a pimp and lives this fairytale life pimpin with snowflake. They take a trip and finds out just what the real world has to offer. Over the years the young minded self-proclaimed pimp realizes that he was never meant to be what he started off trying to be. And becomes much much more at the cost of losing his only family . . .

What would you do if a total stranger hands you a black bag and says "I'll see you when i see u!", than drives off? Well that's exactly what happened to me years ago in Vegas . . . It was never meant for me not to be in your life. Over the years I've done nothing but wonder each and every single day if you were ok. Seeing you laying here like this hurts my soul, but you deserve to know how everything happened and why. I guess I'll start from the beginning . . . .

SECTION 1

I'D BE LYING if i said I was an ordinary guy, when the truth is I'm so far from ordinary. Honestly! I feel like I should be a tourist attraction or something. I mean look at me! Young, fly, stay iced out, always fresh, keep plenty of hoes around me and all i do is get money. Laugh my ass off! Ok, I might as well keep it 100. True enough I'm young, but my jewelry didn't cost as much as it looks. I'm fresh as hell but this shit str8 knock-off! I got one hoe, only good thing about that is she's a snow bunny. She be on some boyfriend girlfriend shit and all I want to do is get some mo hoes and make a whole bunch of doe.

"Baby! . . . . baby! . . . . P! . . . . I know you hear me calling you!"

"I hear you, but you aint saying shit."

"O, ok, I forgot. Daddie, you ready to take me to work?"

"Alday! Let's get it."

"What are you going to be doing while I'm working baby?"

"Try to knock some hoes, like i do every day."

"Is that all you think about? And I'm not your hoe. I'm your girlfriend and you're my man!"

"Alday."

"Why is that your answer for everything?"

Damn I can't wait to get this bitch out her car!

"The lot looking kind of good, you got some regulars coming tonight?"

"O my god! Every time you say some to me it's about money. I told you I hate that! You don't care about me at all!"

"Yes i do snowflake. Without you there is no me baby, come on now. You know I'm just trying to get this business up and going so you want have to do this no mo."

"Yea whatever, just at least act like you love me."

"Alday baby, I love you."

"Yea you better, and yes i have a few regulars coming. You know i got this. Don't be fucking no hoes either especially not in my car!"

"Alday."

"Bye!"

(slams door)

"Biatch!!!" (turns up music)

I'm so tired of living in Memphis. I can't wait to get away from here. Every day the same thing. Drop the hoe off, come back home and sleep. Maybe hit a bitch, than hit the strip clubs. I'm so tired of fucking with these tired as hoes! (phone rings)

"What the biz is?"

"Baby some guy in here wants to give me 3,000 to come back to his hotel with him tonight. He's from Las Vegas, and he wants me to work at his friend club down there. What you want me to do?"

"Is that a trick question? Get that doe!"

"What if he wants to have sex with me?"

"For 3 stacks? You better drop them draws!"

"Are you serious!?"

"Alday, text me what hotel y'all go to."

"You love me?"

"Alday baby."

"I knew you were going to say that, bye!"

3 stacks, damn rite you better hoe up for that. Fuck you mean. I hope he not bullshiting about that money. Hold on let me text this hoe "get that money first!" Alday, sounds like its gone be a good night. I'm ready to hit the club now. Naw, I need to make sure my hoe straight.

(text comes through)

"We're at the Marriot downtown. Room 412, and he gave me 1500 at the club."

"Well you need the other 1500"

"DUHH!"

I'ma smack that hoe! Smart ass mouth!

"I'm parked on the lot!"

Damn, I than fell asleep in this car. People walking pass looking at me. Hell you looking at lady, how you doing (nodding his head). (text comes through)

"Coming down."
"You get the money?"(no response)
I know this hoe see me texting her.
(car door opens)
"I told you that's all you care about is money and not me! Here! (Crying)."
"Baby why you crying?"
"Because i can't believe you made me do that. I'm never doing it again so don't ask!"
"Alday."

She aint talking bout nothing. 3 stacks came out the deal.
"I'm hungry! And I don't want fast food either!"
"Alday baby, you wanna go to Waffle House?"
"Yes daddie (with a smile on her face)".
"You know I love you baby. You're the only family i really have. It's just you and me".
"Alday daddie".
"alday baby".

"Baby you remember the guy from Vegas last week?"
"Alday, Mr. 3 stacks. What about him?"
"He texting me asking If I'm coming or not. I told him I'll need some money to get there. He said he has another 3,000 for me."
"Damn what he do?"
"Well he said he helps run some of the casinos down there. I think he with the mob or something."
"Why you say that?"
"Just the way he was talking the other night. He really likes me."
"You trying to make me jealous or something?"
"(smiling) No baby, he just does. Everybody likes me."
"Yea whatever, tell him to send the money than and we gone."
"Ok daddie".

It's something up with dude. I gotta watch him. But damn, Vegas is where it's at. I'm too ready to roll. I'ma keep my cool though. I don't trust nobody, I gotta watch her ass to. I can't believe dude dropping money off like that. He must got some popping. If I had it I wouldn't be tricking it off with any hoes. I'm glad he is though, I ain't mad at him at all. I'm not turning down no doe, that's for damn show. It just sounds too good to be true. He might be trying to knock me for my hoe, and if he got that money she might just leave my ass for dead down there. Or she might stay down, but that's a nice size might. I gotta get my game tight and knock some hoes while I'm down there. I wonder what's in store for pimpin when I get there. Vegas might not be ready for me. Shid I hope I'm ready for Vegas. What I'm I saying? I'm ready for anything, especially when it comes to that money.

"Baby he buying me a ticket and sending the money. We just have to get you a ticket and we gone. You proud of me baby?"

"Alday snowflake. Let's get it!"

SECTION 2

"I CAN TELL YOU'VE never been on a plane before (smiling)."

"Why you say that snowflake?"

"Because all five of your finger prints are still in my little arm (starts smiling)"

"Alday my first time. How many times have you been on a plane?"

"Not that many maybe five times."

"Without me? You can't do that anymore!"

"(smiles) ok daddie never again without you. I promise."

"I can't believe we in Vegas. I never believed I'd be here this soon at my age."

"Baby how old are you? Why you want tell me your age or anything about you before we met?"

"Because snowflake I didn't start living until I met you and my age doesn't matter, never really have with me."

"Well I wouldn't care if you were 100yrs old. I'd still love you the same. That want ever change no matter what happens. I'd do just about anything for you."

"Alday baby, I know you would."

"What time you meeting Mr. Three stacks?"

"O, um, I'm not. All I have to do is just go to work daddie. The money should be three times better here, and the club just a few miles away from here. I can catch a cab."

"We need a whip baby. I gotta be able to get to you if something goes wrong."

"(Laughing and smiling) You mean get to your money?"

"Alday that to, but no you means no money so I'd rather be getting to you to make sure you're safe."

Damn good come back P, that's right. You in Vegas, step that game up.

"Yea ok daddie, that's why I love you so much."

"Alday, now let's get to it."

"Alday daddie (smiling)."

Life has taught me a lot of things. Especially how it would try to knock you down, but I'm getting back up every time! Being in a foster home didn't break me, family not wanting me didn't break me. Streets can't break me. What else you gone throw at me God? I feel like i can take the world. (With a serious look on his face) (Than smiles) I can't take it from this hotel room though. I been cooped up for a week now. I got like twelve stacks here. It's time to step out and see what Vegas got going. Damn, baby might call the room and need me. Some told me not to trust cricket phones out here. Nationwide coverage my ass. Fuck it, I'm out.

"Were to sir?"

"You know what cab driver, that's a good question. I'm not from here. Just drive for now i guess, something might catch my eye."

"Anything specific you're looking for?"

"Alday, I need to get fresh ass hell, and then hit a few strip clubs. Any clothing stores around here so a north Memphis pimp like me can do it big?"

"Aw you're from Memphis, I see. I know just the place. (Gets on his phone speaking Italian)."

"Alday, let's get it."

Man this a big place. Damn look at them white hoes.

"Ah cab driver where they going?"

"O, those are working girls. You ready to spend big money to be with them? (Smiling and laughing)."

"Hell naw Jack! Are they ready to make big money for me is the question. Stop the cab! I need to get at them hoes!"

"No no just relax. I'm taking you where you need to be."

"Naw pimpin, with them hoes is were i need to be right now. Stop the damn (cuts me off with a gun in my face)"

"Shut the fuck up! We been looking for you."

"You just gone put a pistol in my face like that?! Fuck you mean looking for me? I don't even know you white boy!"

I can't believe this nigga got a gun in my face. What the hell I than got myself into?! I knew I should've just stayed at the room!

"Don't worry P! I know who you are!"

"Man look I ain't with that taking ass shit. You gone have to kill me homie, you got me fucked up!"

"Taking ass (starts laughing) that's funny. Shut the fuck up!"

"Fuck you sucka!"

(Pulls up behind a building in front of a limo) "So you're P?"

"Alday, I don't sign autographs either pimpin!"

"(In Italian) I don't like you!"

"Speak English motherfucka!"

(Throws a black bag out the limo)

"What the hell is that yo sleeping bag?"

"I'll see you when I see you. For your sake you better hope that's never again. Leave! You ever come to my city again, I'll kill you."

"I gotta get my girl first you Italian bread and meatball cracker sandwich eating motherfucka!"

"Forget the girl, she's already dead!"

(Limo pulls off)

"Get in the cab!"

"Where you taking me homeboy?! I need to pack my clothes."

"You're already packed and ready to go. My advice to you is never come back, or he will kill you!"

"Fuck yall! I been dead all my life homie. What yall trying to do ain't scaring me. Were my hoe at?"

"He already told you! She's dead! GET THE FUCK OUT!!! My cab sir."

"Where the fuck I'm I?!"

"Out skirts of Nevada (cab burns rubber away)."

WHAT. THE. FUCK. JUST HAPPENED! Damn, they killed my hoe? This shit unreal, I gotta be dreaming. She can't be dead! She was the only family i had and they just gone take her like that. Naw, I can't go out like that! But what the hell can I do about it? I'm just one person. Them bitches got a whole cab company obviously. (A tear runs down his face). Damn baby, I really did love you. What I'ma do now? I don't even know where I am.

(Loud truck horn)

"Baby you look to good to get hit just standing in the street like that."

"Doesn't matter, maybe I'll feel better after you hit me."

"(She starts laughing) sounds like you're from down south. Country slang"

"Alday cute face, you heading that way?"

"No I'm dropping a load off in L.A. You need a ride?"

"To L.A? Alday, why not. I've never been there befoe."

"Before, don't you mean never been there before? (Starts smiling) come on baby jump in."

"Thank you. Never had the pleasure of meeting a female truck driver. Are you a lesbian?"

"(busts out laughing) No sweetie I'm married with two baby girls. And the names Angie, but everybody calls me Ann."

"Nice to meet you Ann. I'm Percy, everybody calls me P."

"So, P what's your story honey?"

"Actually my book starts now. In L.A I guess."

"How old are you P? You seem mature but your eyes tell me different."

"You mind if I take a nap? It's been a long day; I need to rest my mind."

"Sure darling you can set your bag in the back if you like."

"Alday."

"All day? What does that mean sweetie?"

"Just means ok or I agree, depending on the conversation."

"O, ok than. (Smiling)"

(P falls asleep).

"Wake up darling."

"How long have I been out?"

"Well you've been snoring for a few hours now (laughing)"

"(Smiles) I apologize for that."

"No no its ok, reminds me of my husband. You had to been tired. Who is Fran?"

"Excuse me?"

"O, you were talking in your sleep about some girl name Fran."

"O, an old girlfriend."

"O, ok are you hungry?"

"Alday. I can buy us some to eat. It's the least I can do."

"Sounds good to me. Theirs a shower in the Truck Stop if you need it sweetheart

(Opening the door getting out the truck)."

"Alday, let me grab a towel out my bag. (Unzips the bag)

What. The. Fuck!!!

"You say something honey?"

"No! No! I'm ok. I'll be in, in a second."

"As you say, all day.

(Laughing walking off)" These all hundreds!!! Fifty thousand dollar stacks, twenty stacks means that's. HELL NAWW!!! (With the biggest smile ever). These twelve stacks in my pocket might as well be twelve dollars compared to

this! Why! What?! Fuck that P, don't none of that matter rite now! Just stay cool and calm down. Think! Think! Alday, just keep heading to L.A.

"How much do truck drivers make if you don't mind me asking?"

"Well that depends on the load and how many miles you have to haul it. It pays the bills. You thinking about being a truck driver?" "Actually I'm thinking I'll never work again, not like I ever have anyway but I wanna start a business. You think your boss makes a lot of money?"

"(starts laughing) my boss has nothing to worry about. His employees have made him millions!"

"How much would it cost to start you think?"

"Well you have to buy trucks, a ware house, and trailers and start getting contracts. Maybe, a good 150k should get the ball rolling, why you ask?"

"Wanna be my business partner?"

"(Laughs) sure sweetie, now where are we getting that kind of money darling?"

"A family member passed and left me a lot of money and I'm ready to start a business. Right now."

"Right now? Just like that? Well how much did this family member leave you?"

"More than enough!
(Smiling)"

SECTION 3

LIKE I SAID before, life is crazy. Ann and I have been in business together for a few years now. She's been like a mom to me; she even took me to get my first driver license. She was so shocked when she finally found out how old I was. I've done more traveling and networking in the last few years than the average business man will probly do in ten years. I've flown out the country six times before I was old enough to buy beer out the store, even though I don't drink nor do i smoke for that matter. I started off trying to be a pimp to try and get to where I am now, which would've took a life time at the rate I was going. But honestly, I miss her. I've never once stopped thinking about her, not even for one second.

I live kind of good. I have a nice house, Hummer, Escalade, G-wagon, Range Rover, Bentley Gt Coupe', Porsche Truck and a few toys. S.S Impala on 26inch rims, Road master on 24s and a Yacht that I never get in because I don't like the water. Some other things in Paris, Canada and Miami of course. I own a few carwashes in Miami and two Adult Gentlemen clubs. A chain of restaurants in L.A, Arizona, Flagstaff and Houston. That black bag is worth awhole lot more now. But I'm still alone, afraid to get close to another woman again. I haven't even been back to Memphis or Vegas at all. But I am, you better believe that!

(On the phone)

"Hey Ann, how's everything going on that end?"

"Great P! Everything is looking good considering we just signed with three more companies, so we're still rolling."

"That's good, that's good. How's the family?"

"Everybody's just wonderful, they ask about you all the time."

"Alday, I'll be there for Christmas and new years. I'm working on something else now; it's going to be real major. Especially for the economy."

"There you go again, all work and no play. You need to relax sweetie. You're one of the richest young men I know at age 24. You should enjoy that, settle down and start a family. You still just sleeping around or will we be meeting someone when you come to visit?"

"(Laughs) You know me."

"Yes I do, and that means you're still just sleeping around."

"Alday. Well I'll see you next week for Christmas."

"Ok darling be careful. I love you P."

"Alday, I love you to."

(News broadcast)

"This just in, Multi-Millionaire Percy Palmer was shot four times in a carjacking while leaving one of his night clubs in Miami. Police tracked the Bentley Gt down using on star and arrested two men in connection with the shooting. It was said that Palmer had twelve thousand in his vehicle and the money has not yet been recovered. Police are still looking for suspects. Palmer is listed in critical condition, and doctors say the next few hours aren't looking good for the 25 year old millionaire. Representatives of Fran Truck and Hauling Company are offering twenty thousand for the black bag containing the twelve thousand that was in the car, as crazy as it sounds. More on the story as it develops."

Damn! Four times! What the hell was I thinking not being strapped? I guess that's what I get for thinking like a business man and not like I'm from north Memphis. God if you can hear me, I want to fight this. I feel I still have a higher purpose here beyond the money. I've changed my life for the better at least that's what I was hoping I was doing. But if you feel it's my time than your will be done.

(Monitors beeping)

"Hey Ann, how long have I been out?"

"(crying with a smile) Baby you've been snoring for about a week now (starts laughing) I thought I lost you darling."

"It's gone take a little more than that to take me out; did they get my bag back?"

"Yes, the police recovered it from a third shooter, with the money still in it. I know how much that bag means to you."

"Alday, what's the damage to my body?"

"Well the doctors say the surgery went well. All the bullets were removed, but you lost a kidney. The other is holding up just fine. It's going to take a while for you to recover and start back walking again. But you're going to be fine sweetie."

"Alday"

"You're blessed son. It was like God had his hands on you."

"He has been there all my life, that's what I've come to realize."

"They said your age on the news (smiling)."

"Are you serious?"

"Yep, everybody knows now, no more living low key, the word is out."

"It was gone get out sooner or later I guess. Just didn't expect it to be like this.

Did anybody come to see me?"

"I'm sorry darling (shaking her head)."

"Doesn't matter, you're my only family. I really appreciate you Ann. You've been there for me since day one."

"No P, thank you. Without you I'd still be driving trucks, away from my family all the time. You're part of my family now and always will be. All day? (Laughing)."

"Alday Ann, I love you."

"I love you to son. My brother has a cabin in the mountains. I want you to stay with him until you're better and I want take no for an answer."

"Ok, mom (smiling)."

(Speaking Italian)

"Hey boss have you seen the papers?"

"Of course I have, were is Francheska?"

"Out back with her son. She hasn't heard about it yet."

"Good, keep it that way (blows cigar smoke)."

"It's going to be tuff keeping her away from the news and the papers boss."

"(Looks with a sharp look in his eyes)"

"Ok boss, I'll handle it."

"(Stands in the window smoking a cigar, watching Fran and the boy)"

(Somewhere in the mountains)

"You're up walking around pretty good and sooner than expected."

"Alday, I don't do well just laying around for some reason."

"All day (laughs) my sister told me about that word."

"Are all these metals yours?"

"All day (smiling)."

"How long were you in the service?"

"Twenty years. Then I retired and I've been with the C.I.A for five years now."

"C.I.A. So that means you can fight and shoot really good huh?"

"Among other things, yes (laughing)."

"Can you teach me?"

"(laughs and smiles) All day."

"Alday, let's get it. (With a serious look on my face)."

SECTION 4

(TRAINING IN THE mountains)

I guess it's true what they say. Everything happens for a reason. If I wouldn't have been leaving the foster home that day I wouldn't have met Fran. If I wouldn't have told her to do that date with Mr. three stacks, we wouldn't have went to Vegas. Then I wouldn't have had the black bag or lost her. Never wouldn't have gotten shot, well at least not in Miami. And I never would've met Mike. He has trained my mind as well as my senses. I've exercised mentally, learned how to handle and maintain weapons. Learned martial arts and how to survive off the land, as well as bomb and ammunition training. I feel like one of those guys in the movies now. Mike offered me a job with the C.I.A. I took the test and passed, actually I'm top three in my class of 42. I've been with the unit for two years and 7 months now. Working as team leader under Mike. As agent Palmer. Code name Agent P.

"Palmer I need to see you in my office."
"Yes mamm."
"Close the door behind you please."
"You wanted to see me Captain?"
"Yes I did (with a smile on her face) unbuckle your pants!"
"Yes mamm!
(With a smile on my face)"

I've been seeing the Captain for the past six months now. Professional well educated woman, but she said I bring out the caged freak in her. You know how I get down; I'm still from North Memphis now let's not forget that.

"Baby I hope you brought the right suit this time. I can't be leaving out your office with different clothes on."

"Yes daddie I did (smiling)."

"Alday."

"Now the real reason I called you in here is because I have a situation in a small city in Italy. Complete black opps. The briefing folder is under your naked (smiling) sexy ass, Agent P."

"Alday Captain I'll take care of it."

(Somewhere in Italy)

You know I bet other agents wonder how I always get my orders directly from the top when Agent McClain (mike) is my superior and he takes his orders from her to give to me so I can pass it down. (Laughing) Same old Pimpin just a different type of mind that listen. Anyway my orders are to observe and report. I can't believe there's no hit list this time; she knows how I love those. The file is labeled priority so I'll handle with care.

(Camera snapping pictures)

I wonder what these guys are into. Could be drugs, really could be anything. My last few assignments were all different. (Continues snapping pics) (Focuses in on the driver) Hold on! I know this guy! That's the cab driver from Vegas. Mr. Gun in my face! What is he doing here? Only one way to find out. I wonder where he's heading, because I know where he's about to end up. (Smiling) Nobodies going to miss a cab driver.

"Wake up Mr. cab driver. (SMACK!) Wake yo punk ass up! I bet you never thought you'd see me again?"

"(speaks Italian) i don't know what you're talking about."

"Of course you know what I'm talking about (in Italian) and I already know you can speak English very well."

"P? Is that you? My my how you've grown, and speaking Italian to. I'm impressed."

"Well, as you can see your balls are connected to this car battery. Every time I push this button (starts shocking him) you get a tingling sensation. So start talking!"

"(breathing really hard) Francheska is still alive! (In Italian)"

"What you mean still alive? What's going on old man?"

"The boss thought she was too good for you. And you had to go."

"What boss? The guy in the limo?"

"(Breathing hard, not talking)"

"Alday, have it your way (pushes the button again)"

"Ok! Ok! Ok! Yes! Yes! He is the boss. He runs all of Vegas. He is her father!"

"Her father?"

"Yes! We received word she was working in Memphis at a strip club, so he sent me to get her. But she refused, because of you. Only when you had enough money she said, she would come home than. So I gave her money at the hotel to give you."

"Hold on, hold on! You're Mr. Three stacks?"

"I gave her three thousand to give you if that's what you're asking, yes. And she still refused. The boss told her he would have you killed if she didn't come to Vegas. And she brought you. We looked everywhere for you when she made it to Vegas, than you popped up in my cab."

"So what's up with the black bag?"

"Pay-off, to stay out her life!"

"Conversation over home boy! (Pushes the button and walks off).

Damn! Why did I kill him before I asked what they tell her about me? All this time I've been thinking one thing and it's been the total opposite, I can't believe that. (Smiles) They thought they didn't like me than, wait till they see the new P! It's time to go back to Vegas. It's been ten years, I wonder if she even remembers me. What if she's married? Doesn't matter, it's the boss I'm after now. Alday.

(Back at headquarters)

"Here's your report Captain. I need permission to do a special assignment Captain."

"What's the nature of the problem?"

"It's personal Captain. Unfinished business."

"Now you know I can't officially authorize that Agent Palmer."

"(clears his throat) Can you do it for daddie?"

"(Smiles) take a week off Agent."

"Thank you captain."

"And P . . . . be careful."

"Alday Captain."

SECTION 5

(AT P'S HOUSE) I can't believe this woman is still alive! (Breathing hard hitting punching bag) I thought that life was behind me, and now this! I have to stay focus. I'm not the same guy I use to be! She was still my family and they took her away from me! (Still hitting bag) Somebodies got to pay for that!!! (Hits bag one last time!)

(House speaks)
"Sir, thermal scans indicate a vehicle is approaching."
"How many body heat signatures?"
"Only one sir."
"Face recognition?"
"Scanning . . . . Captain Brittany Davis sir."
"Let her in."

"Welcome Captain Davis, P is in the bed room shower. Please make yourself at home and enjoy your stay."

"(surprised look on her face) Umm, thank you. (Goes into the bedroom, takes her clothes off and gets in the shower with P) Hey daddie."

"I was hoping to see you tonight

(Pulls her close. shower water hits their bodies as they kiss) (Female moans and soft screams are all you hear throughout the bedroom)

"I don't know what it is about you baby, ahhh! ooow . . . P don't stop daddie! I'm Cumming baby

(She whispers). I'm Cumming baby (even louder) ooooOOOOOO!!!!!!!!! (She screams, breathing hard) ooh shit baby! I can't feel my legs!"

"(P smiles) that's because I have them in my arms."

"You know you're the first woman that's been in this bed?"
"Yea right, are you serious?"
"(smiles) you're laying on my chest snowflake, can't you feel my heart rate?"

"(Listens for a minute) Yea I guess you're telling the truth. You have so much going on for yourself, why haven't you settled down with anyone?"

"It's really hard for me to trust someone. I've been abandoned, and lied to so much, I just figured I'm better off alone. Besides, I wouldn't really know how to treat a woman like a woman."

"Whatever! You're so smooth and laid back; I know you get all the girls. (Smiling)"

"It's crazy because at one point in time, I was trying to get all the girls and wasn't really paying attention to the one I had because I was too focused on money. Then I got the money at the cost of losing the girl."

"Well now you have money and me, that's if you want me."

"Are you serious?"

"(smiles) can't you feel my heart rate?"

"Alday baby. I have to close a chapter in my life first."

"Well as you say P, all day."

"Sir, 7 vehicles has stopped less than 100 meters from the house."

"(P wakes up out his sleep) How many heat signatures?"

"16 approaching sir."

"(Getting up grabbing weapons) Face recognition?"

"Scanning . . . . negative sir."

"Move all images and signatures to my Pad and go stealth mode now!"

"What's going on baby?"

"I'm not sure. You have your weapon?"

"Of course!"

"Alday, here (throws here a thermal heat scanner) anything red is not us. I'm going to the back stay here."

"Be careful baby"

"You to! (Thermal scans show they've breeched the house. P slips throughout the house. First 3 guys are taking out instantly. Without shots fired! Here's shots! Stab to the throat drops another one. Head shot head shot! Two to the heart! Neck snap! Arm break three shots to the chest!)

"I'm out!"

(P throws her an M-2 grenade launcher. BOOM! Cocks back BOOM!! P takes heavy fire, he dives behind a cabinet. Shots to the legs bring them down. Shot to the chest one to the head)

"All clear?"

. . . . "All clear! You ok snowflake?"

"I'm good, you?"

"I'll be better when I find out who the hell sent these clowns. House!"

"Yes sir."

"Thermal scan"

"Scanning . . . . 18 scans 2 heart beats."

"Take his mask off. Face recognition."

"Scanning . . . . Vincent Marino a.k.a Vinnie the snake. Affiliation: Jezeppih Family."

"Jezeppih family? Why would they be here, they're the reason I sent you to Italy. They've been extorting money from Vegas for years and we've been trying to get the boss!"

"The boss . . . . His ass is mine!!!

"What do you have to do with this P?"

"Don't worry about it, I'll handle it."

"No! Baby you have to tell me how you're involved."

"What would you do if a total stranger pulls up on you, throws a black bag out a limo and says I'll see you when I see you and drives off? That's exactly what happened to me 10 years ago!"

"You took money from them?"

"More like threatened and forced is more like it. They took the only family I had, and now it's time to take theirs!"

They have no idea who they're fucking with. Come in my house and try to kill me! Too bad they made one mistake! I'm still alive! (Goes to a gun cage in his house and grabs all type of weapons, grenades, explosives and any and everything!) I really didn't think I'd ever have to come down here to this room, but life is crazy like that. Everything has led up to rite now. Life or death! But if I go, I'm taking a few heads with me!

(Phone ringing) "Hello"

"Hey what's up Ann is everything ok?"

"Of course darling, what's wrong?"

"I'm outside your home."

"Outside? Why didn't you come in? I'm coming out sweetie."

"Ann, you know you've been like a mother to me. I want you to have this."

"What's this darling?"

"Power of attorney over all my businesses and accounts."

"(With a worried look on her face) why are you giving me this?"

"Cause you're the only family I have, and where I'm going. I might not make it out."

"You know P; I've watched you grow into someone very special. Your life isn't what it used to be. You don't have to do this you know."

"These few years have been a blessing, meeting you was the best thing that's ever happened to me. I have to finish what they started, before someone I love gets hurt. I love you Ann."

"I love you to P! You be careful and come back home to me son."

"Alday"

(Phone rings) "McClain."

"Hey Mike, I need a big favor!"

"No problem I heard what happened, you ready to handle that?" "Alday, let's get it"

SECTION 6

(IN THE WOODS outside the boss's house in Vegas)

"You know this might be suicide rite P?"

"You trained me. You don't believe in me now?"

"Just be careful and watch your back. Here's the building layout you asked for, but why did you want it on a flash drive?"

"So house can tell me how many people are inside and show me exactly were everybody is."

"House?"

"Alday, High-tech observation using special equipment. H.O.U.S.E. I've uploaded C.I.A files to it for face recognition and other things."

"I have to get me one of those."

"(smiles) I haven't put it on the market yet. One of a kind baby. If I'm not back in 20mins, I'm dead."

"I'll see you in 19mins than."

"Alday."

(house scans the property)

"17 rooms, 28 thermal heat signatures, 12 security cameras and 6 active alarms."

"House, disarm all alarms in exactly 60 seconds, than arm them again 12 seconds after that on my mark . . . Mark! (runs across the grass, takes out three guards and takes one of their radios. Climbs to the second floor, cuts a hole in a window and enters the building)."

"(hear guards speaking Italian)"

"(hears a female voice coming down the hallway) P, were are you honey? (in Italian)"

"(snatches the girl) (speaks Italian)

Please don't scream I'm not here to hurt you (covering her mouth) who did you just call? (still speaking Italian)"

"My son, please don't hurt him (soundind scared and worried) he is just ten and is hiding from me, please don't hurt us. Please. (crying)." "I'm not here

to hurt you. I want to help. I'm with the government, do you want out? This whole operation is about to go down."

"I've always wanted out! We have to find my son! Please!"

"Ok, let's go. (pulls out house and shows her the floor plans) doesn't seem like anybody is in this area. Find the boy and meet me here quick as you can ok."

"Ok, but who are you?"

"Some one that wants to help, now go!"

Change of plans. I need to get them out of here. I'll deal with the boss later. (hears Italian guards talking, walking towards his way) (speaking Italian)

"What you mean nobody made it out alive? Get back here now!"

That was Mr Three stacks. No wonder those guys came to my place. That's ok next time I'll make sure you're dead! Believe that.

"Hey you! Who are you? (in Italian)" "Your worst nitemare (bullet to the head). Time to go!" "Did you hear that? Francheska, go! Find her, now!! (Italian)" "Yes boss!" "Now!!!"

"Come on snowflake we gotta roll"

"Snowflake?"

"Come on little man let's go! (in Italian)."

"Mike, I'm coming out the back, I need you to cover me."

"I got you P! (talking through the ear piece)."

"(runs out the back with the boy in his arms and Fran trailing behind) (Italian guards coming out shooting!) (A.k rounds rip through the guards from the woods) (P makes it to the truck with the boy and Fran)"

Put your seatbelts on and hold on to something! (in Italian) Mike all clear, I'm out!"

"Ok, I'll see you back at H.Q"

"(pulls in a near by airfield and boards a private Jet.)

"Where are you taking us?"

"You speak English."

"Of course I do, but you didn't answer my question!"

"Some place safe snowflake."

"Why do you keep calling me that? That's not my name sir."

"I apologize miss, what's your name?"

"Francheska. What's yours?"

"Agent Palmer, I work for the C.I.A."

"I haven't been in a plane in a long time Agent Palmer. And my son has never been in one. You have anything to eat for him so he can relax?"

"Sure everything except chocolate (opens a cabinet)."

"Good he is allergic to chocolate for some reason."

"So I'm I, there isn't any on this plane at all trust me."

"I trust no one!"

"Alday."

"Excuse me? What did you just say?"

I said why don't you trust anyone?"

"Someone I knew a long time ago taught me that, before he died."

"How did he die?"

"You know you ask alot of questions Agent Palmer, but he was killed."

"Alday."

"I knew it!"

"Knew what?"

"Where did you get that word from? You stole it, it doesn't belong to you. Why do you use it?"

"I've used that word my entire life snowflake . . ."

"O my god! . . . P? (with tears coming to her eyes)"

"Alday baby"

"(grabs him and starts crying)."

(plane lands in Paris)

"Wake up snowflake, we're here. (picks up the boy and carries him to the truck)" "Whose house is this P?"

"Yours snowflake."

"What you mean mines? Wait a minute, weren't you speaking Italian a few hours ago (with a smile on her face)."

"Not only do I speak Italian (in Italian) I speak nine other languages also (sounding cocky)."

"(starts laughing) How many hoes have you pimped to get all of this? (smiling)"

"I've never in my life pimped a hoe, I've had a girlfriend once that helped me get money. And I've missed her everyday since the last time I saw her."

"You still have good game P, I'll give you that. Are you married, any kids or baby mamas? (smiling looking around the house)."

"(laughs) No. No and no. Not that I'm aware of. What about you? Are you married to the kid's father?"

"No, I haven't spoken to his father in awhile now. I've raised him all on my own. He speaks a little English but mainly Italian. My father forbidded him to learn English."

"Cute kid."

"His name is Percy."

"(looks at her with a strange look) You named him after me?"

"He's your son P. I never knew your last name so he has mine. I really didn't know much about you other than I would've done anything for you, and that I was in love with you!"

"(P just looks at the boy) House."

"Yes sir." (Fran jumps and looks around stunned by the voice)"

"I need you to run a dna comparison."

"Yes sir. Samples please . . . Thank you. Scanning . . . . Dna matches 99.999 percent comparison."

"You didn't believe me (smiling) o, I forgot. You don't trust anyone."

"(P grabs her, holds her and kisses her) Come with me. (leads her to the bedroom) He will be ok in here. House let me know when my son's heat signature starts moving around the room."

"Yes sir."

(Italian boss) "How could you let this happen?! I want my daughter and grandson back now!!! (slamming his fists on the desk) and I want P DEAD! Do you understand?! DEAD!!! (in Italian)."

(back at P's house) "I have something to show you. Look in that black bag."

"What's this?"

"Well that bag is what your father gave me before telling me he killed you and to never come back to Vegas. The money is the same twelve thousand you made before all of this happened. Check the years, I never spent one dime of it."

"You know my father told me he killed you and had you buried in the dessert. I never spoke to him again after that. I'm so sorry for lying to you daddy but I was protecting you. My father is a very powerful man. That's why I ran away, than I met you."

"Yea I had a talk with Mr. three stacks in Italy. He told me about it."

"(laughing and smiling) Mr. three stacks? O, you mean my uncle. Yea he does all my father's dirty work. Are you going to arrest them?" "Well I'm not in

the business of arresting snowflake. That's not my specialty. But yes, something will happen to them."

"I don't care, they've hurt alot of people. They deserve what's coming."

"Alday."

"What's this? (looking at some blue prints)"

"Plans for my new business. If everything goes rite it should employ over four thousand people in the U.S alone. I've been working on it for awhile now."

"I guess you were really trying to start a business back than."

"Alday, but this one is yours."

"Mine? I wouldn't know how to run a business, especially one this big."

"I mean look at me (smiles) I was 18 calling myself pimpin,"

"You were only 18? (laughing and smiling)"

"Alday, started my first company before I was 20 now I own over 14 companies across the country. I have other people running them, but that's because I don't like the spotlight."

"(busts out laughing) Since when? From what I remember you love attention!"

"I've changed alot snowflake."

"I see (smiling).

"The boy is now awake sir."

"Come on."

"(speaks Italian) mommy were are we? Who is he?"

"My name is Percy little man (in Italian)"

"My name is Percy too. I'm ten and a half years old. My birthday is in three more days, isn't it mommie? (holding up three fingers)"

"Yes baby."

"He's so smart."

"Just like his father."

"I can't believe I have a son (looking into the boy's eyes)"

"This is your father P."

"My father, really? I thought you told me he went away?"

"I did go away son, but I promise I'll never leave you like that again. I give you my word ok."

"Pinky swear?"

"(busts out laughing) Pinky swear."

(phone rings) "Hey Ann, I'm glad you called. You won't believe this."

"(speaks Italian) If you ever want to see her again, bring the boy and Fran back to Vegas! You have three days..! (phone hangs up)

SECTION 7

"I KNEW I SHOULD'VE killed him!"

"Who?"

"You know who. This time he's crossed the line!"

"What's going on P?"

"He kidnapped a family member for the last time! He's going to kill her in 3 days If I don't bring you back to Vegas."

"Than you know what you have to do! (with a serious but sad look)"

"Alday, I know exactly what I'm going to do!

(phone rings) "They got Ann Mike! They say she's dead in three days If I don't return the girl and the boy."

"Meet me at the cabin. Now!"

"Alday. (Bentley motor switches over to overdrive)

"What does my sister have to do with this P? And who is the woman and the boy?"

"The boy is my son Mike."

"Son! I thought you didn't have any family, how the hell is that your son?"

"Look, we can stand here and argue all niter, but time is running out! And taking them back is not an option Mike!"

"Ok. This guy wants a war, that's exactly what he's going to get! Get the hell out my way P!"

"Look Mike, she's my family to! The only mother I've ever known. We're going to get her back together. Alive!"

"For their sake, she better be alive."

"I'm bringing the team in on this one. I don't want to take any chances."

"Mike you know this is a one man extraction."

"I don't want to leave anything to chance. Besides I want to make sure there's no one left to come back after her."

"Alday, Lets get it."

(back at P's house) "Mommie why are you crying (in Italian)"

"Your grandfather is going to go away P. We may never see him again baby."

"Yes we will. Grandpa said he will always be around, no matter what or where we go."

"That's what I'm afraid of."

"Vehicle approaching, waiting for face recognition . . . . Agent Davis."

(doorbell rings)

"Go in the back baby until I come and get you ok."

"Yes ma'am."

(goes to the door)

"Yes, may I help you (in Italian)"

"Yes, I'm Captain Brittany Davis with the C.I.A (shows badge) I was sent here to get you. (with a smile on her face)"

(outside of Vegas) "Ok, everybody has their objective. Let's execute this one like professionals ladies and gentlemen. One clean sweep." (over the radio)"

"Sir theirs a government vehicle approaching the house."

"Are you sure? Confirm."

"Positive sir, just pulled into the garage."

"Copy that. What the hell is going on."

"Let me go in first sir, give me ten minutes exactly."

"Ok. Be careful Agent P. Bring her out safely."

"Alday."

"Here's the girl back like I said. How did she get mixed up with one of my Agents, and who is she?"

(pointing at Ann with something over her head)

"Where is the boy!?"

"What boy? You didn't say anything about a boy! And who is she for the last time!?"

"That's Angela McClain, P's business partner."

"(clears her throat) Did you just say McClain? I have to get out of here! How could you be so stupid!"

"We needed her to get the boss's daughter back, we couldn't trust you to do it. And you still didn't get the boy!"

"(shaking her head) If that's who I think it is, P and a few other agents are already here!(sounding a little scared)"

"(light's go out) You've made a big mistake Captain! How could you betray us like this. How could you betray me like that!?"

"It never would've worked out P! You just had to ruin everything, why couldn't you just have forgotten about her and loved me? We would've been great together P (pointing a gun at Fran's head) This bitch messed everything up! You here me?!!! (lights come back on and Ann is gone)

"Were did she go?! (in Italian)"

"Come on honey let's go! (pulling Fran by the hair)"

"Were do you think you going with the boss's daughter? (real quick in Italian)"

"(shoots him in the head) Out of my way! Let's go! (pushing Fran into the hallway) (Mike and the other Agents move-in)

"Did he make love to you and play with your mind to? I bet that's the first thing he did when he got you back wasn't it? (with the gun still pointed to her head trying to get to the truck) That's rite, you better not answer that!"

"I don't see what he saw in you from the beginning (in Italian)"

"(smacks Fran across the head with the gun) Shut up bitch! (in Italian)"

"Why are you doing this Captain? Is it for money?"

"Show yourself P, or I'll kill her. Don't test me!"

"I'm rite here. Baby how did you get wrapped up with these people? You can talk to me."

"There you go P, always trying to get in the woman's head. (with tears running down here face) I fell in love with you P! Why did you have to bring her back into the picture? You had the money I didn't need the Italians anymore."

"Is that what this is about, money? I have a million dollars in a black bag outside in my truck. You can have it, just let her go."

"See P, you don't care about me. You're to in love with her. Why can't I be you rite now? (looking at Fran crying)"

"Francheska! (yelling in Italian as the guy shoots the captain from behind)"

"Nooo!!! (P shoots the guy three times in the chest)

"I loved you P. I wasn't trying to fall for you but I couldn't help it. (coughing, bleeding out her mouth) But I knew we would never be. I knew you wouldn't love me back." "You didn't give me a chance to baby. I was getting there (holding her head in his arms) But you would've been another disappoint in my life I see. I sensed something was wrong. That's why I took my time with you."

"(with her last breath) I'm sorry daddy."

"Alday."

"P! You ok?"

"Alday Sir. Did we get the boss (helping Fran off the ground)"

"No, he was never here. So the captain was the leak. Never thought it was her."

"You knew somebody was working for them?"

"Of course, you can't keep dodging the C.I.A without having one of them on your payroll. We've been trying to shut their operation down for years."

"Why didn't you tell me sir?"

"Couldn't risk it."

"Hay darling."

"Ann? You're in on this to?"

"Yes honey, It wasn't faith that put you in my truck that night son, but over the years you've found your way into my heart darling."

"In a matter of moments you've found your way out of mine. (with a disappointing look) Is Mike even your real brother?"

"(takes a deep breath) No. I work for the government to. Not even the captain knew I was undercover. Nobody but Mike and our superiors. But I never once lied about caring for you son."

"DON'T CALL ME SON! (eyes fire red) All this time you've been using me and I was thinking I had a real family."

"I apologize P. I was doing my job."

"Alday. And I'm going to do mine!. (throws his badge on the ground, grab Fran's hand and leaves)

"Are you ok baby?"

"All my life I've been lied to. I don't know what's real and what's not now. Where's my son?"

"She never saw him he's still at the house. Probly worried, scared and crying."

"House, bring up video footage. There he is, asleep. (sees a man walk in the room) Who is that?"

"O NO!!! That's my father!!!"

SECTION 8

(AT HEADQUARTERS) "WHERE is he?"

"Who?"

"The uncle, the number two man. I saw him in cuffs before I left, where is he?"

"You through your shield in P, I can't let you talk to him. You know that already."

"Listen Mike, they have my son. (with a serious look on his face) You owe me!"

"(sighs) Interrogation room 3. You have 5 minutes."

"I'll only need 2."

(interrogation room with Mr. Three stacks) "Where is my son?!"

"(laughs) What makes you think I will help you?"

"Last time I didn't stick around to see you die, but the sound of this grenade going off will assure me your done this time! (pulls a grenade out his pocket) What's it gone be?"

"You can't do that you're the police now, they want allow it (sounding a little nervous)"

"F.Y.I I quit! I can do whatever I want now, and I know how to get away with it! Talk!"

"I don't know where he is, I thought he was with you! I've been here (sweating looking at the grenade)"

"Last chance, once I pull this pin six seconds and boom!!!"

"I'm telling you I don't know! Please! It was never my idea to take them from the beginning! Please!!!"

"(pulls the pin)"

"Ok Ok!!! Without Francheska he has no power over Vegas."

"(puts pin back in the grenade) Keep talking."

"His wife's brother is head of the Rizzuto family and he was murdered. Only blood can take over. Francesca's mother passed years ago so that meant

Francesca was next in line to give Massino (the boss) power over the Rizzuto family. Now that you have her, guess who's going to take over now."

"My son."

"Exactly. If that happens he has control over Nevada, New York and most of the crime boss's in Italy. That's going to be all bad for alot of people! (with a smile on his face)"

"Why is that so important to him?"

"(laughs) Power!"

"Trust me he doesn't want the boy that would take to long. He wants his daughter. Bad! He wanted to kill you so bad. I was the one that asked him to spare you, and look how you treat me."

"Does Fran know about any of this?"

"No, just by her showing up he would be recognized as the head boss. But she always refused to get on a plane or even leave Vegas for that matter. As far as where your son is, he could be anywhere. There's alot of protection around him right now. Practically untouchable. (smiling)" "Trust, he's about to be touched real soon. (walks out)

"What did he tell you P?"

"Why? I can't trust you. As far as I'm concerned you know where my son is. How could you and Ann do me like that? (smiles) You know what, doesn't matter to me anymore. Just stay out my way Mike!"

"P we want to help."

"Man get your hands off me! You've done enough!"

"Look! We gave you a life."

"You gave me lies! What type of life is based on lies? Obviously the one I've been living! Stay out my way!"

My life has been flipped all the way upside down. I can't trust anybody, the family I thought that was my family isn't really my family. My family is part of the mob and missing. What the hell I'm I going to do? (serious look on his face) I'm getting my son back!

"Snowflake think real hard. Where do you think your father could've taken him?"

"I'm not sure. I never got involved with him like that to know about all the places he has been or would go. I'm sorry baby."

"At least we know he want be hurt with him."

"That's not true. People try to kill him all the time. His life is constantly in danger because people don't want him to gain the power that I have."

"You know about that?"

"I've always known. My mother told me about it when I was a little girl. Rite before she died she told me that's why my father married her. For the power. I think he had her brother killed to."

"What if you took over, than what would that mean?"

"Nothing. The families wouldn't really respect a woman like they would a man."

"Why is that? I think if you demanded respect you would get it."

"But that's not the life I want P. I never wanted to be a part of that."

"You wouldn't at the expense of getting our son back? Cause if you don't, that's the life he's going to be exposed to."

"We have to do what we have to do. I'll be there with you every step."

"(busts out laughing) A black man and a woman taking over the world's largest mob . . . You must have a death wish or something because nobody is going to like that. Everybody will be at our heads!."

"I'm ready! Are you? I want my son back. I'm ready for whatever."

"Are you sure?" "Alday!"

"We're going to have to make a name for ourselves and get a Borgata."

"What's that again?"

"Some loyal soldiers baby. It's going to be hard finding those. Almost impossible!"

"We have to make it possible."

"I know a few guys that I probably can trust if the price is right."

"Well money is one thing I have plenty of so that won't be a problem."

"We're going to have to commit alot of crimes to baby. Are you sure you want to do this?"

"Alday. Whatever it takes. What kind of crimes? Extortion, robbery (pauses for a minute) maybe even murder. The life of a crime boss is exactly what it sounds like. Crime's boss."

"How will we know when we are respected by the other families?"

"We want know. Honestly we have to be prepared to never be respected. That's why we're going to take it by force! Francheska Rizzuto. My name has to speak for itself."

"What about my name?"

"Want mean jack to the Italians baby. You're going to be like my hit man. The hired help. My Button as they would say. Someone I call to perform an execution."

"Alday."

It took me two days to learn the Italian mob's lingo, and how they operate. Discussing it wouldn't prepare me for the life I was about to step into next. I can't believe I'm about to go from a C.I.A agent to a Capo dei capi. I wish! I black man being the boss of all bosses would never happen! Besides Fran was going to be the boss. I could only be an associate because I'm African American.

A crime boss is a person in charge of a criminal organization. A boss typically has unquestioned command over his subordinates, is greatly feared by his subordinates for his ruthlessness and willingness to take lives in order to exert his influence, and profits greatly from the criminal endeavors his organization engages in.

There is a typical structure which crime organizations may operate under. The Mafia, being a very prominent example, is not the only one. The typical structure is usually as follows:

**Boss - Also known as the Don, "capo crimini," or "family patriarch," this is the highest level in the criminal organization.*

** Underboss - Also known as the "capo bastone" in some criminal organizations, this individual is the second-in-command. The underboss is sometimes a family member, such as a son, who will take over the family if the don is sick, killed, or sent to prison. He is responsible for ensuring that profits from criminal enterprises flow up to the boss, and generally oversees the selection of the caporegime and soldier(s) to carry out murders.*

** Consigliere - Also known as an advisor or "right-hand man," a consigliere is a counselor to the boss of a crime family. The boss, underboss, and consigliere constitute a three-man ruling panel, or "Administration." The consigliere is third ranked in the hierarchy but does not have capos or soldiers working for him. Like the boss, there is usually only one consigliere per criminal organization.*

** Caporegime - Also known as a captain, skipper, capo, or "crew chief," the caporegime was originally known as a "capodecina" (captain of ten) because he oversaw only 10 soldiers. In more recent times, the caporegime may oversee as many soldiers as he can efficiently control.*

** Soldato - Also known as a sgarrista, soldier, "button man," "made man," "goodfellow," or "wiseguy." This is the lowest level of mobster or gangster. A "soldier" must have taken the omertà (oath of silence), and in some organizations must have killed a person in order to be considered "made." A picciotto is a low-level soldier, usually someone who does the day-to-day work of threatening, beating, and intimidating others.*

** Associate - Also known as a "giovane d'onore" (man of honor), an associate is a person who is not a soldier in a crime family, but works for them and shares in the execution of and profits from the criminal enterprise. In Italian criminal organizations, "associates" are members of the criminal organization who are not of Italian descent. An associate may never rise above this rank; an example of a close associate is Hugh "Apples" MacIntosh of the Colombo Family.*

Some groups may only have as little as two ranks (a boss and his soldiers). Other groups have a more complex, structured organization with many ranks, and structure may vary with cultural background.

"It's time to start our family snowflake."

"Excuse me! The names Donna Zuto!"

"Alday boss. Let's get it!"

"We need to go to Memphis."

"What's in Memphis?"

"My Caporegime! Frankie the Fists is the guy I want. Last time I heard about him he was in Memphis working at his Italian restaurant. He loves money and knows more about the organization than I do. Plus he's not a hot head."

"Who's Next?"

"I know a few soldiers and I'm almost certain Frankie Knows a few good guys. I can't believe we're actually going to do this. For real!." "People do crazy things for family. Sometimes It's not what you want to do, but what you have to do. Life is about choices, and we've made ours Donna Zuto."

"You're rite. I have to get my mind into it. I can handle it."

"I know you can. We're going to find Percy Jr. Than we're going to get away from everything."

"Ok."

SECTION 9

Return To Memphis

"(FRANKIE BUSTS OUT laughing) No disrespect Francesca but no self respectful wise guy out here these days would honor a female boss. It's just not natural."

"They would if they were hungry enough (opens a black bag). You see I happen to know for a fact that their are soldiers out there looking for a home. I'm just the women, correction the boss their looking for."

"there's over fifty grand in this bag."

"I expect you to have your crew ready to meet with me in two weeks. Spread the word. Donna Zuto is no one you want to play with. This Borgato is serious business! It's time to make money, earn respect and make history."

"Are you sure about this? Alot of the other bosses across the country mite not like this."

"Than I'll be more than happy to have a sit down with any boss that has a problem. I'll be sure to bring my problem solver."

"Whatever you say boss."

"(Fran breathing hard) I can't believe I just did that. (thinking to herself) I enjoyed it. (with a smile on her face) I mite get use to being the boss for once. Regardless of who likes it or not. I know this is only for my son but I know the old man want let anything happen to him. Besides this is what's in my blood, It's meant for me to take over. If everything goes rite, as though it should, I'll be one of the most famous women in history. P want like me talking like this at all. But I'm the boss now not him. Once I get the money up he can do what he wants, besides a boss with a blackman probly want workout. I have to worry about what people mite say or think. The other families mite not approve, I'm not even sure if I approve. I haven't seen P in years, and even though we have a son together doesn't mean we are inclined to be a family. Maybe if I would've just listened to my father in the

first place our family would be built by now. I'll have somebody take care of P once the ball gets rolling . . ."

(P drives around Memphis) I can't believe I haven't been back here in over ten years. Doesn't feel like home at all, I haven't even seen any familiar faces. Maybe that's because I stayed to myself so much. I wonder if the same people still work at the youth villages over on poplar. Might as well stop by, It want hurt to check it out. Probly won't even remember anybody.

(at the youth villages) "How are you doing sir, how may I help you?"

"Hello, I'm Percy Palmer. I use to live here."

"Aw, well welcome back (smiles) we rarely have to many people from the program to return after they have left. Feel free to look around if you like."

"Does Mrs. Andrews still work here?"

"You know Mrs. Andrews, of course she's still here. Over forty years now, actually she's runs the program for the state of Tennessee now. She usually stops by around this time. Would you like to wait for her?"

"Yes Ma'am If that's not a problem."

"No problem and please don't call me ma'am makes me feel old. I'm Ms. Robinson."

"Nice to meet you Ms. Robinson you can call me P everybody else does."

"(smiles) How about I call you Percy than since everybody else calls you P."

"Alday (smiles)"

"Not all day just for the time you're here."

"(laughs) No alday just means ok."

"Than why don't you just say ok than Percy (with a flirtatious smile on her face)"

"It's a habit, I've been saying that since before I left here. That's how alot of people know me."

"Sometimes it's not good for alot of people to know you. What's your profession Percy, if you don't mind me asking."

"No I don't mind, and for the last three years I've been working for the Central Intelligence Agency."

"Sounds like the program worked out for you. Some kids leave here and never find themselves, so stuck on the fact that nobody wants them. Most turn to a life of crime, many end up in a cell or in a grave. I wish most would turn out the way you have."

"Well I didn't start off that way. It's been a long journey I've just never given up."

"High spirited. I like that Percy.

What church do you attend Percy?"

"(smiles) I'm almost ashamed to say I've never belonged to a church."

"Yes! You should be ashamed, but nobodies perfect and God knows what's in our hearts. You still should be blessed with the word every Sunday morning. Nothing is more important than the lord. Remember that ok."

"Alday, I mean yes ma'am, I mean ok (smiles). How long have you been working here?"

"I've been here for about two years now. I have a BA in developmental psychology. I like to help these kids develope themselves before we just push them out the door. You know what I mean."

"I wish we had someone like you here back when I was here. Life was hard than."

"But you turned out fine."

"Looks can be deceiving Ms. Robinson. It's not easy."

"Well life isn't easy Percy but with faith and guidance we can prevail."

"You're absolutely right."

"(smiles) I know I am."

"(Mrs. Andrews walks in) Hello how is everybody doing today?"

"Just fine Mrs. Andrews how are you today?"

"I'm blessed to be here I can tell you that. How are you doing young man?"

"I'm Fine Mrs. Andrews, I'm Percy Palmer. You might not remember me but I use to live here."

"O my goodness! (with a smile on her face) Yes I remember you! Come here give me a hug. How have you been? Where have you been?"

"Percy works for the CIA Ms. Andrews."

"Whaaaat! I can't believe it. You've grown so much I barely even noticed you. You were the smallest little thing running around here all shy and now look at you. Come come have a seat tell me more about you."

"Well there really isn't much to tell. My life has been like a movie since I left this place. A few ups a few downs but never any hold backs." "How did you get a government job?"

"Well it's kind of complicated, but I knew somebody that knew somebody else and they trained me. I went to school and got a degree in criminal justice, took the tests required and past them with flying colors. I haven't been here in Memphis in over ten years really."

"Well what brings you back? I know not this old place."

"I'm here on business for a few days. Than I'm heading back home."

"Are you married, any kids?"

"Ms. Robinson why you all in this man's business like that?"

"(P laughs) It's ok. Well I've never been married and I just recently found out I have a ten year old son. But his family doesn't approve of his mother and me."

"She must be white?"

"Um, you have to excuse Ms. Robinson P."

"It's fine. She's actually Italian."

"Aw well I have work to do Mrs. Andrews, It was nice meeting you Percy If you're here Sunday you should come visit my church. Golden Gate on James Road. Do you know where that is?"

"Al (stops himself) Yes I do."

"Good here's my card incase you have any questions. Ill see you later Mrs. Andrews it's time for me to go home and wine down."

"Ok Ms. Robinson you be safe."

"I will."

"So, Percy Palmer all growed up. I'm so proud of you. You just don't know how good it feels to see one of my kids all grown and doing something positive with their life. It is truly a blessing."

"I have a question Mrs. Andrews. Do you know anything about my parents? A name or an address or anything."

"Well it's against policy to disclose that type of information Percy."

"(shakes his head with disappointment)"

"But I'll see what I can do. Let's go in the office. (types on the computer) Percy Palmer, Born in Memphis, Tn in Shelby County. Mother's name unknown. Father's name unknown. Hold on a min let me cross reference a few things here. (continues typing) Here we go. Your mother's name is Regina Palmer. Last known address is listed in Dixie Holmes Apartments, but they have been torn down for years. I'm sorry P but that's all I have."

"A name is more than enough, Thank you I can handle the rest."

"You're welcome P, I hope you find what you're looking for."

"So do I. I'll see you again before I leave Mrs. Andrews I have a few things to tend to."

"I understand Mr. C.I.A you be careful out there Memphis is a crazy place now."

"Alday. But I'm not the same either. I'll talk to you later."

(P calls snowflake) "Hello."

"Hey what's up snowflake, how's everything going on your end?"

"It's actually going good. I have a meeting with a few wise guys later tonight."

"You want me to be there?"

"Umm no I can handle it, Just let me take care of it. Some of those guys mite not want to understand why you're in the meeting."

"Alday, I understand that. Well you be careful and let me know if you need me. You need anything?"

"Probly about a hundred thousand so I can get some things going. I know it may sound like alot but trust me that's pennies compared to what I'm suppose to have."

"Give me a few hours and I'll have it."

"Ok baby. What are you about to do?"

"Get you this money and check on a few things while I'm here. I'll let you know when to meet me."

"ok. I'll talk to you than."

"Alday."

"House, cross reference with the Memphis yellow pages looking for a Regina Palmer. Last know address was 126 Ayers in the Dixie Holmes."

"Scanning . . . . Regina Palmer, last known address is 921 Lewis St. 38106."

That's in north Memphis. Should I go? Why should I? I wanna know why she didn't want me, that would be my first question. I don't want to bust her out in front of anyone. maybe she has a family and doesn't need me coming to mess that up. First things first I need to go to the bank and get this money than I'll see if I really want to deal with seeing her or not. That's alot of money to take out at one time. It's going to draw alot of attention from my old employers, but who cares! I have to find my son and they're not trying to help so fuck'em. I'ma do it my way.

"(Fran and Frankie talking) When was the last time you had somebody whacked?"

"Is that a trick question Donna? What are you asking me?"

"I need someone taking care of tonight. He's dropping off a load of cash and I need him gone after the deal is done. Can your guys handle that?"

"Of course simple work. Just let me know when and where."

"Make sure It's quick and painless. I don't want him to suffer."

"Can't guarantee that but the job will get done."

"Good, make sure they know not to under estimate him. He's a dangerous person."

"Who are we talking about here Steven Siegel?"
"No but he's just as worst."

"I have the money snowflake, where do you wanna meet?"
"By the news station under the old bridge."
"Why in a place like that? What's going on?"
"Nothing I just don't want anybody seeing us together right now."
"Alday. I'll be there in thirty minutes."
"Ok, I'll be waiting."

That's crazy as hell she wants to meet there, What's up with that (P thinks to himself) Maybe It's nothing. Whatever I guess she knows what she's doing.

(under the old Memphis bridge) "I've never been down here before. I hate the way water looks at night. Here's the money."

"P, you know I use to be so crazy about you. Remember when I said I'd do almost anything for you?"

"Alday"

"Well I've found out why I said almost. (three guys walk up with guns pointed)"

"What the hell is this? Your betraying me to, bitch don't you know I'll kill you for this. What about our son?"

"As far as I'm concerned he's in good hands. I can't do what I have to do with you in my life P. (almost wants to tear up) I have to be what I was born to be. The Boss. (takes the money gets in the car and drives off)"

"I can't believe this shit! So yall suppose to kill me or sum? Well what the hell you waiting on! I'm ready! Let's get it!"

(multiple gunshots are heard in the distance)

"Push him in the river! Throw the guns in to. Come on let's get out of here."

SECTION 10

God wants me to be alone

DAMN THIS WATER is cold! Why me God? Every time I think I have a family, you take it away. Why? Should I be happy and satisfied with just money, because if that's the case I don't want it! Maybe I'm suppose to be alone. If that's the case so be it. I'll stay alone, rich and miserable.

(phone rings) "Hello"

"How you doing Ms. Robinson, this is Percy we met earlier at the group home."

"Yes I remember, It's one a.m Mr. Palmer."

"I know but it's an emergency I need your help, I'm standing outside of the gas station across from the Mata bus station dripping soak and wet. Can you come and get me please? I know it's alot to ask but I don't know any one else here in town I can call. Please (sounding desperate)"

"Ok I'm on my way, O Jesus! You just stay right there."

"Alday."

This lady don't know me at all. Why would she get out of her bed to come help me out? I can't answer that but I'm glad she's coming. I look like a bomb standing out here cold as it is soak and wet. I hate the cold weather. First time back in Memphis in over ten years and look what happens. Snowflake orders a hit out on me, I get dumped in the Mississippi and had to swim I know at least two miles maybe three, all the way down to Harbor Town. I'm glad I know I can't trust anyone! Something said P, wear your vest. Glad I listened.

"Looks like you need a ride sir!"

"Yes mamm I'm afraid I do. (getting in the truck) Thank you so much, my rental car is parked down under the old bridge."

"I'm almost afraid to ask why it's down there and you're down here, but I got out my bed at one a.m. I think I deserve to know, don't you?"

"Well it's complicated."

"Try me"

"Ok, well my old girlfriend who I thought was dead (goes on about what happened, not telling the whole story) than I was suppose to meet her under the bridge, next thing I know I'm getting shot and throwed into the river."

"(unbelievable look on her face) You expect me to believe that Percy?"

"I told you it was complicated."

"Please get out (with a smile on her face) where are you staying tonight, well for the rest of the morning sir?"

"I'll find a hotel."

"Dripping wet like that, I don't think so. Follow me, I'll get you fixed up."

"You sure, because I can take it from here."

"Yes I'm sure now let's go it's cold out here."

(at Ms. Robinson's house) "Here's some pants and a t-shirt to put on, hand me those wet clothes."

"Do you always help strangers and bring them back to your home?"

"O yes all the time (sounding sarcastic). I honestly don't know why I got up out my bed (putting out a blanket on the sofa) and drove across town to pick up a man I don't even know and now housing him. That right there should show you how good God is."

"Thank you so much, I've never had anyone do anything like this for me before. Without it being a setup."

"Well if I was gone set you up I would've did it from bed and left you standing out there in the cold. Let me take a look at those bruises." "Their just impact wounds, nothing serious."

"I don't know what kind of life you've been living to say getting shot and thrown in a river is nothing serious. Are you going to call the police?"

"Why would I do that? They can't help me."

"Well what about your C.I.A friends I know they can help."

"I have no friends. Everyone betrayed me, Everyone I've ever let in my life. I trust no one."

"Well you can trust God! He will never let you down. He might not be there when you want him to be, but he's always right on time." "That's some faith you have."

"All it takes is a little mustard seed of what I have to know God is our father and whatever problems you take to him he handles accordingly."

"I've never even been to a church."

"Say what?! Never been to church!"

"Nope. Not once."

"Well that's why you feel the way you do Percy. You've never been touched by the word!"

(they talk on into the morning until the sun raises)

"Here you go. (brings P breakfast)"

"Why are you being so nice to me? Did you see me on t.v or something?"

"(starts laughing) My God teaches me to be this way and who are you for me to be than seen on t.v?"

"Nobody, I was just wondering. What do I owe you for all of this."

"Just a little of your time Sunday morning at church."

"Are you serious?"

"All day! (with a smile on her face). Trust me It'll make you feel better."

"You know I trust no one."

"Percy, you can always put your trust in the Lord Jesus Christ. All you need is a little faith."

"Faith than taught me one thing. God wants me to be alone."

"That's so sad. Your eyes say alot about you. Shows you have a soul and a good heart. Having those qualities you should know you're never alone in the presence of the Lord."

"Maybe church will make me feel better, cause hearing those words felt like a chill going thru my bones."

"That my friend, is the presence of the Lord."

Once again I'm in a life changing situation. How could Snowflake have done me like that? There was no reason to cross me. Was she put up to it or was it all her? Why? Unanswered questions are what kept me going this long. I felt so good at church today really it doesn't matter anymore. It was like the pastor was talking directly to me. Learn to forgive, let it go and live. I've never lived a normal life. I really don't even know what normal feels like or where to start. Sounds like Ariel, knows how to start. I'm going to do the one thing I've never done in my whole entire existence. Put it in God's hands.

(two months later) Haven't heard or seen Snowflake in over two months now. I could've easily found her by now, but why should I. I've been enjoying my life where I am so far. In the back of my mind I want my son back, but It seems like with me in the picture his life is in constant change. I don't want

that. I actually enjoy spending time with Ariel. We've been doing alot together, especially going to church. Makes sure I'm there every Sunday. Feels like that's what I really need.

(Ariel and P out on a date) "Ok I've been letting you win all night, it's my time now. (smiling)"

"Letting me win? Shooting pool is what I do (laughing) and no game having men like yourself, always say the same thing."

"O, you come here often with different men huh?"

"No you're the only man that wants to spend time with me like this doing something I enjoy."

"I'm enjoying it also. How about we play next game for a question?"

"What you mean?"

"Whoever wins gets to ask the other one a question and you have to answer it truthfully."

"You mean you've been lying all the other times (smiles)?"

"Look are you in or out?"

"I'm in, let's do it."

"You won, your brake." (no balls go in)

"You might have a chance this game."

(P never misses one shot) (Ariel stands there with her mouth open)

"Looks like I won."

"You're real funny you know that. I guess you have been letting me win."

(she turns around and sees P on his knees)

"Will you marry me Ariel Nicole Robinson?"

(speechless)

"I know we really don't know to much about each other but I feel like you're what I've been waiting for my whole life and I wanna do it the right way. That's if you'll have me."

"Yes . . . Yes!. Yes! I will marry you. (crying and smiling) (P puts the ring on her finger and she grabs him and kisses him for the first time)." (P smiles) I knew that would be worth the wait. (everyone in the pool hall starts clapping and cheering).

I don't know what I'm doing, but It feels right. I love this woman! And that's what I'm going to show her. Every day of our life from here on out.

"By the way, did I mention I was rich? (with a smile on his face)"

"What you mean rich?"

"I mean rich, as in I have a nice size bank account. You'll be proud of what I've accomplished in my life."

"I'm already proud of you now just by excepting the lord into your life."

"Alday."

"I knew you were gone say that. (and they kiss).

SECTION 11

WOULD YOU BELIEVE me. Of all people would have a family of my own. My beautiful wife and I have been married for twenty two years now. We have a son named Tyler that's in law school now. He has a good head on his shoulders, I've tried my best to give him what I never had. Real people that love him unconditionally. Most of my companies I've sold but that's only because I've started new ones. I have this major corporation called Global Office. We supply every major electronic, office supply and computer software warehouse across the globe. Of course I'm the C.E.O, I actually work and live a normal life. All glory and phrase go to the good lord above. My office is in New York of course, the capital of business networking. It's a little complex, because we live in Lansing Michigan. I take a helicopter from the roof, to the airport to board a jet, that takes me to my vehicle parked, at Lansing C. R. International. Than I drive home. Everyday. I can't say that I'm fully happy, but I am blessed.

"Percy I wish you'd tell me where we were going or at least let me take off this blind fold."

"We're almost there just be patient and enjoy the ride. You don't like the way the plane feels soaring thru the air? It's suppose to relax you while I feed you baby, now relax and open wide."

"Ummm, baby that taste great, why you don't cook this all the time?"

"That's an easy one, everyday is not as special as this one."

"(blushes) Twenty two years and you still have good game baby."

"Alday."

(Jet lands and a limo takes them to this bar)

"You ready for this?"

"Finally baby yes."

"Happy anniversary beautiful. You remember this place?"

"O' my god. Isn't this were you proposed to me? (smiling)"

"Of course it is, you didn't think I'd let them close this place did you. I bought it a few years back when the owner wanted to sell it and now it belongs to us. Have a seat my Queen. (pulling her chair out)"

"Thank you."

"You know what Mrs. Palmer, I was hoping there was something special about you every since we first met. God lead me to you. My whole life has been tested, preparing me to meet you one day. Having your love over the years is God's way of saying you passed Percy. (Waiter pops a bottle of champagne and pours them both a glass) To us beautiful twenty two years, and looking forward to the next twenty two."

"(tears start falling from Ariel's eyes) I love you Baby."

"I love you to beautiful. Don't cry baby, is that your way of telling me you're scared to see me on the pool table?"

"Please, aint nobody scared of you.(smiling) You just get some quarters.

(back in Michigan) "Hey Ty where you headed tonight?"

"Home! (smiling) I have to much studying to do. I don't see how you guys party all night and be in class the next day. It has to be something wrong with that."

"whatever man you study to much, you should have fun every now and than."

"This is law school my friend the best studied even harder. I'll catch you later, be careful out there."

"Ok man see you tomorrow."

"Alday."

(Tyler walks to his car)

"LISTEN ONE WORD AND ILL BLOW YOUR BRAINS ALL OVER THE PAVEMENT DO YOU UNDERSTAND NODE YOUR HEAD"

(Tyler nodes his head yes)

"Good, now get in the car." (they drive off).

(cell phone rings)

"(laughing) I told you, you didn't want this."

"Whatever lucky shot, hold on for a second cheater. Hello,"

"(Tyler reads this note) "Dad I have been kidnapped and unless you pay one million in cash in twenty four hours I will be dead! This is not a joke and they mean business. You will be contacting with instructions on where to bring the money! (phone hangs up)"

"(P stands there stirring at his wife.) What's wrong baby, who was that?"

"Somebody kidnapped Ty"

"What? Who? What you mean kidnapped Percy don't play with me! (with a serious look on her face.)"

"I wish it was a joke (holding her) They said give them a million dollars in twenty four hours or he's dead. Don't worry I'll get him back!" "Please baby get our baby boy back (crying) please."

(phone rings) "Hello"

"Hey Mike this is Percy I need your help."

"Agent Palmer It's been along time."

"Cut the small talk I'm headed up to your office now call down the clearance. (Hangs the phone up)"

(P comes into the office)

"How you been doing P?"

"Look cut the small talk I need your help, my son has been kidnapped."

"Sounds like you need the police."

"Are you serious! You don't think you owe me this one?"

"Look that was a long time ago P and you walked out on us."

"Mike. Did you not just hear me, they took my son, they took my son. Will you help me or not?"

(stands there looking at Mike in his eyes)"

"When was he taking?"

"About five hours ago. They gave me twenty four hours to pay a million or he's dead. Now anybody that knows me know I could have that faster than they can count it. Why give me twenty four hours."

"Don't worry we'll find out. Whose your son been hanging out with?"

"Nobody that I can think of. All he does is study, he never goes or does anything. See if you can pull a name from the last call to my cell. (walking out the office) and get me a badge and a gun. I need full access to the computers and new data."

"You got it."

"H.o.u.s.e upload all new data files from the hard drive."

"Yes sir uploading . . . . upload complete."

(goes thru files and messages from Tyler's face book page looking up friends)

14hrs 32mins before deadline.

(Talks to teachers and students at his school. Looks up backgrounds off all Global office employees) "Another deadend!"

"How you holding up baby?"
(on the phone crying)
"Im not, knowing our boy is out there with people that are doing God knows what to him . . . My baby wasn't prepared for all of this Percy why would somebody do this to us?"
"It's going to be ok baby I'll get him home safe I promise. Have I ever made a promise I couldn't keep?"
"(still crying) No. Don't let me down now either Percy please don't let them hurt him."
"I want."

6hrs 13mins left before deadline.

(phone rings) (reading from a paper)
"Dad It's me. Don't talk just listen. Bring the money to this location in five hours alone and unarmed. If anything goes wrong for any reason (pauses for a min) I am dead!"
"Don't worry son I'm going to bring you home! (trying to hurry up and say before they hang the phone up). H.o.u.s.e trace that call."
"Yes sir scanning . . . . address found."
"Vegas . . . . I know she didn't. How would she even know. Time to find out."

(grabs the black bag with the money inside it)

3hrs 17mins before deadline

(P goes thru the back door of a warehouse.)
(here's some guys talking)
(sneaks around looking for Tyler)
(Steps out and grabs one of the guys)

"One Move and you're dead! Where's my son?"

"(Speaks Italian) I don't know where he is. You where suppose to get those instructions after you dropped the money off."

"Where is he, Is he here?"

"No! He doesn't know where he is. I do!"

"Who are you?"

"Don't you recognize me? Come on now It hasn't been that long . . . . Look at this guy everybody! (speaking Italian) This is suppose to be my Father. The infamous P everybody!"

"Jr?"

"That's P Zutto to you, none of that Jr garbage Capesh."

"Why are you doing this son? Don't you know that's your brother you have."

"Course I know! Can you believe this guy. It's a shame the kid doesn't know about me. Now why is that might I wonder. Hummm maybe because his father forgot to tell him over the years aw yea son you have a brother out there in the criminal world somewhere, but don't worry he's a grease ball forget about him."

"It's not like that son."

"(raises his voice) Don't ever call me that again you understand!"

"Where's Tyler?"

"O he's around, did you bring the money?"

"Of course! It's rite there. I could've given you that the same day, why wait twenty four hours?"

"O trust me I wouldn't have given you ten minutes, The twenty four hour thing wasn't my idea."

"Whose was it? Your mom's?"

"I want to kill you rite now! Donna Zutto was murdered almost seven years ago."

"Did you have anything to do with that?"

"Are you kidding me, I'm pretty sure you know exactly who was responsible for that?"

(Big door opens and a black truck drives in)

"Here's little Tyler now. We're about to be one big family!"

"(lights are to bright can't see who gets out the truck. A guy grabs Tyler out the back and walks in front of the truck. Mike! What the fuck are you doing?"

"What do you mean what Im I doing Agent Palmer it's time for me to retire. It felt only right to cash out now. Besides a million dollars not going to hurt you at all. Your worth billions and look I've even brought the family back together. How could you abandon a son P? I thought your situation would've taught you better than that."

"I didn't abandon him he was stolen from me! Than his mother betrayed me while we were trying to get him back."

"Is that why you killed her?"

"Killed her? Is that what you're telling him? I haven't seen Fran since she left me to die in the river."

"Wait a minute I thought you said you asked for five hundred thousand. You lying piece of shit you trying to cross me out?

(P jr pulls a gun out on Mike)"

"Put that thing away son I was being gracias giving you half of that. Now put the gun down before somebody gets hurt."

"He didn't even know my mother was dead! You told me he was the one that killed her to get revenge. And I've told you about that son bullshit!!!

"Who you gone trust him? The guy that left you for dead and never came back. Didn't even have the guts to tell your only brother about you. Or you gone believe me, I'm the one that been there for you since your grandfather was murdered."

"Don't listen to him P He's been lying to you! I went through hell to get you and your mother back once I found out she was still alive. Your grandfather told me he killed her before you was even born. I found the both of you and they took you again when you were only ten years old. Now he's lied to me before I know how persuasive he can be but you have to believe me."

"Aw fuck this! (Mike shots P jr)

(The other Italians start shooting at Mike hitting Tyler in the arm)

(Mike let's go of Tyler grabs the bag and takes off running.)

"Are you ok Ty?"

"Yea dad It's not that bad check on him."

"(P jr coughing and bleeding really bad) I can't believe all these years I thought you abandoned me and killed my mother.

(coughing)"

"Don't talk. I've never once stopped thinking about you son."

"I hate it when people call me that."

"Don't worry I'll get you both out of here."

(P puts Ty and P jr in the truck and drives to a hospital near by.)

(doctor walks out in the waiting room)

"How are they doctor?"

"We removed the bullet out of Tyler's arm successfully, but the bullet we removed from Percy punctured his right lung and he lost alot of blood. The next few hours aren't looking good."

"Listen to me I need the best doctors in there working on my son here is my insurance card I don't care what it cost just save my son!"

"I apologize sir but money cant save his life only God can."

(The doctor walks out)

(P walks in Tyler room)

"How are you doing son?"

"I'm good dad. Just never been shot before, I have to tell you It's not a good feeling."

"Trust me I know."

"How's my brother? The doctor said It's not looking to good. Prayer is what he needs now."

"I've been doing that since I got snatched. It's been working so far, I have faith it will keep working."

"(P hands him a phone) Call your mother she's worried sick about you. I'm going to check on P jr."

"Alday dad."

(the nurse in P jr room is checking his vitals)

"How's he doing?"

"The machine is doing all the work for now, but he seems to have a strong will to live. Still It's to early to tell."

"Can he hear me?"

"He's heavily sedated but doesn't hurt to talk to him anyway. I'll leave you two alone."

"Thank you.

"Hey son, I don't know if you can hear me or not. I've always wondered where you were and if you was ok. I never meant for you to grow up without me, I know first hand how that feels. There was a time when I thought maybe you were better off without me in your life. That was only because I feared you might get hurt. You ended up getting hurt anyway after all of that. I know there's no way to replace or fill in the gaps time has left between us but your still my son. I want to be in your life rite now just like I always wanted to be since I first found out I had a son. Lord please look over my boy, I'd trade places with him in an instant. Just let him experience what it feels like to have a father. Please Lord."

SECTION 12

"HERE'S THE SUITCASE *you asked for baby, where's my son?"*

"He's in room 316. I.C.U. With his brother."

"Brother? What brother? You mean P Jr, how did he get here?"

"It's along story; I haven't even gotten all the details down yet."

"Mom! (Ty grabs his mother and hugs her)

"I thought I'd never see you again! (crying) Are you ok!"

"I'm fine momma; Dad P Jr's waking up! come on."

"Jr, how are you feeling son?"

"Where I'm I?

"You're in a hospital in Vegas."

"Vegas! It's not safe here you have to leave now! If they know I'm here they will come for me, Get them away from here now!!! (starts coughing)"

"Who are they? And trust me all of you are safer with me. It's going to be ok son."

"Stop calling me that and just get them away from here now!!! Listen to me; trust me they will blow this whole building up if they have to! I'm the last blood line in the family and they want what I know and me dead!"

"Baby take Tyler and get on the jet I'll tell the pilot where to take you. Call me when you make it ok. I love you both!"

"We love you to baby. Please be careful! I really wish you'd come with us but I know you want! Thanks for getting our son back like you promised."

"Alday! Now go baby!"

"I got to get out of here soon as possible! You should've left with your family."

"You're my family to! And you're in no condition to leave now."

"I've been in worst conditions trust me. You have to get me out of here. I'm almost certain they already know I'm here and probly heading to this room as we speak!"

I don't know what P jr has gotten himself into but I'm his father it's my job to protect him. I haven't killed anyone in years but the instinct is still there, I've never stopped feeling it.

(four Italian guys enter the hospital and start heading towards the I.C.U)

"H.O.U.S.E patch into the hospital's security systems and bring up the cameras from all the entrances and this hallway."

"We're sitting ducks. We don't even have any weapons."

(Opens his suitcase)
"I see you gone have to learn about me and how I really get down . . . Son . . ."
(pulls out two dessert eagles and a glock 9 19)

"That's what I'm talking about. You might just be related to me after all. We still need to get out of here rite now."

"Hold on. Are these the guys you're talking about?"

"Damn! We got to go!"

"First of all we never run from a fight. I'm old but my wisdom supersedes any youth any day."

(the Italians come into the room and starts shooting at the bed, P steps out the closet grabs the first guy and snaps his neck, using him as a shield shots the other three guys in the head)

"Still got it! Come on Jr let's go (helping him out the bathroom down the hall and into the truck. Searches the truck for explosives and pulls off) You wan to tell me what's going on now. Why are those guys after you and who are they?"

"First of all as you already know I'm only half Italian. That doesn't sit to well with other families that want what my grandfather and mother built up over the years. They feel like I should be killed so pure bloods can assume position and take what my family started. I'm not having that! My life has been in constant danger since I was 16. That will never change and neither will I. You can just take me to my soldiers and I can manage from there."

"Are you kidding me your suppose to still be hooked up to a machine. I'm taking you somewhere I know you'll be safe and you can get your strength back first."

"I don't need your help!"

"Doesn't matter. Until you can get away on your own your stuck with me. Point blank now deal with it."

"Where we going?"

"To a cabin in the mountains. No one will find you there. Plus I need to check on a few things."

(P jr starts coughing, as he wakes up in a strange bed)
"Where I'm I?"

"This is the place that saved my life son. Mike brought me here after I was shoot at one of my strip clubs in Miami."

"Don't call me son and you have a strip club. Mr. Businessman, number three in Forbes magazine. Is that how you became a billionaire, strippers?"

"You know I use to think that strippers would make me rich one day. Before I met your mom my whole thought pattern was all wrong. Your grandfather changed my life completely you know. Without him I wouldn't be were I am today."

"You sure, cause from what he use to tell me he hated you. He said you ruined everything he had set in place for my mom. I always thought it was just because you were black. My mom did the impossible. Started her own family and made millions. My cousin wants to take over now, that's why I have people trying to kill me. And he's connected with the government some how."

"The government has always been tied with the Mob bosses; it's been that way since before I started working for them. How did you and Mike get hooked up?"

"He saved my life. He was there when my grandfather was killed, he got me out alive. That's when he told me you killed my mother. I've been ready to kill you every since. He was using me since day one. Revenge in my heart had my mind cloudy. For years he's been watching my back, giving me information about you and where you were."

"Trust me I know how it feels to be lied to and betrayed. I've killed a lot of people in my life but they all deserved it. I didn't even know Snowflake was dead until you said something about it. I'm going to find Mike and your cousin and see what's really going on."

"I don't need your help you know."

"Alday. But you have no choice."

SECTION 13

The Truth

(ENTER P ZUTTO'S cousin; Don double R)

"Where's P Jr?"

"We tried boss but some of my guys were ambushed at the hospital. He had like 100 guys watching his room, feds and wise guys. Now he's gone."

"Feds? You think he got to them already?"

"I don't know boss it's possible, and if he has that's bad news for us."

"I can't believe this half breed has managed to shake me and my guys all these years. All this power he has and hasn't once used it until now. Why is that; Why now. This whole thing of ours could crumble if the information he has got into the wrong hands. No families would last out on the streets without him."

"He's family boss I don't think he'd do us like that"

"Family! He's nothing but a nigga that's infiltrated our bloodline! A half-breed! Ah ah a wannabe! Don't talk to me about family, family is the reason I don't have the government eating out of the palm of my hands right now at this very instant. You want to talk about family, than get your ass out there and go find this so called family of mine capes!"

"Capes . . ."

(Back in the mountains)

"So what do you call that, karate?"

"No son it's a little more complex than that. Anybody can do karate but it takes perfection to master what I know. I can teach you if you're willing to learn."

"Don't waste your breath, I've never ran into a problem I couldn't fix"

"You mean like your cousin?"

"How bout you watch your fucking mouth, you don't know me! This guy has all the families on the east and west coast after me. Not to mention the government. That's a problem that can't be fixed since Donna Zuttos gone. Smart guy."

"What your mom has to do with this?"

"Everything! She controlled everything and everybody with what she stole from the big guy."

"Which was?"

"Now that's a stupid question. Don't you think if I knew that Id possibly know were to look or even know why they wanted it so bad?"

"You mean to tell me you don't even know why these people are after you?"

"Not a freaking clue. But they think I have it and that's how I like it. At least until I find out what it is."

"How can I help?"

"You can't. That's what I've been telling you. You can let me be on my way, that's what you can do. Besides you have a family to get back to."

"You are my family son when are you gone realize that? Why do you think I'm here?"

"Because I kidnapped your son that's why. You wouldn't be here if it wasn't for that lets be for real here. I've been dead to you. You didn't know if I was living or breathing so let's keep it that way."

"Some times I wish I could go back in time and change my life completely, but that's wrong of me because I have a beautiful family. You're still my family to and if you don't know what you're looking for than we will find it together. You don't have to live this life. All you have to do is say word and I can give you awhole new life without the drama."

"I was born into drama, the way I see it I'll die with drama. My blood alone has enough drama for 100 life times, but you wouldn't understand that."

"If you only knew. At least you had somebody growing up. I had nothing and nobody as a child and most of my adult life. We both have had it hard and I don't regret any of it because it made me what and who I am today. And nothing on God's green earth can change the fact that no matter what my blood flows through your veins too. Never forget that."

"Trust me nobody will ever let me forget about that."

"Good! Now we have to find out what's so special about what everybody is looking for. Where do we start?"

"I've searched all over trying to figure that out. She didn't tell you anything? She was so in love with you I'm almost certain she told you something."

"Nothing I can remember really. You said the government wants you to. I might know somebody that can help with that part. I haven't talked to her in years now seems like the best time for a reunion."

"You trust her?"

"I trust no one son but God. Let's go."

"I thought I told you never to call me on this phone grease ball. I'm out! What part of that didn't you understand?"

"First of all, you're out, when I say you're out! Capes! Second, you were supposed to deliver me this half breed cousin of mine and I haven't seen any progress towards that agent McClain!"

"He's with P now. His father. He use to be with the agency."

"Good, than we have goods on him to."

"Wrong! Agent Palmer quit. He's clean as a whistle, and the wrong type of guy to fuck with. I trained him myself."

"Than he's no good, just like you. I want him NOW! I don't know how much clearer I have to be about this situation. Don't forget Mike, you still work for me now."

"I worked for the big guy; if you were half the boss he was we wouldn't be in this situation."

"You think you can't be touched I see. Take a look out your window."

(Truck explodes)

"What the! . . . How did you even know where I was?"

"Now you listen here you piece of shit! P Zutto, I want him, and his nigger father, Kill'em. Capes!

(Phone hangs up)

"I haven't seen that face in years, how you been doing Ann?"

"I'm still breathing. I thought you had forgotten about me. I haven't heard from you."

"You broke my heart that day. You were like a mother to me. The only woman I thought I could trust."

"That was my job P; I had to do what I had to do. And so did you. I've changed your life in so many different ways, you have no idea."

"What do you mean?"

"The black bag, where is it? Tell me you still have it."

"I've always had it, but what does the bag have to with anything?"

"P Zutto, I haven't seen you in years."

"Likewise."

"You two know each other?"

"She use to work with Donna Zutto. I remember her face, but I don't know her like that."

"I'm the reason Fran had the government eating out the palm of her hand. She knew certain things and details about what the agency was doing. Thanks

to me. You see when the agency assonated my brother I made it my business to see them exposed for everything."

"What does that have to do with me?"

"Well when you got shoot and I recovered your bag I put everything that would expose the government on a disc and sewed it in the bottom of your bag. I knew they would never look there for it. Instead they've been taking orders from the mob thinking they have it."

"And my mom's death?"

"They figured Fran and your grandfather where the only two that knew about anything, so they had them killed. Mike killed them both."

"Mike! I knew I should've killed that son of a bitch. Where is he?"

"Calm down son. What's on the disc?"

"Everything! Assassinations, payoffs, setups and Presidents."

"What you mean Presidents?"

"Every President is picked way before any campaign or election. Votes don't count, the agency does. It's all for show."

"And what do you want me to do with it?"

"I want you to do what you've always done and that's be yourself. If anyone finds out about this your whole family will be murdered."

"Anything else I need to know?"

(A sniper shots Ann in the head)

"Get down son, down!"

"This day just gets better and better."

(P returns fire)

"Mike! I know it's you, you piece of shit!"

"Another family reunion, don't you just love get togethers agent Palmer."

"I'm gone kill this guy!"

"Son wait, come back!"

"You know there's no getting away from the agency agent P. We practically run the world. And the next one that we've been building."

"What you mean the next world?"

"Well agent P it's no secret this world is about to destroy itself. Well man has already destroyed most of it. This whole place is hell and it's going to burn. The sun P, it's coming, you better believe that and I for one don't plan on being here when it arrives."

"You sound crazy Mike. What dope have you been smoking? Why did you kill Ann?"

"Let's see why did I kill Ann, well same reason I killed everybody else. Collateral damage. All you have to do is hand over whatever it is you have and I'm gone."

"You don't know what I have?"

"Not really and I could careless, I just know a lot of people want it including the agency and I have to have it."

(Three shoots are fired)

"I told you I was going to kill you."

"Wait son, wait!!"

(Explosion. A grenade goes off)

"NOOOOO!!!! Jr!"

(P starts crying)

A lot of people have lost their lives, including my son. All this time I've had the one thing that everybody wanted but had no clue as to what it was. You know how dangerous that makes me since I now have and know what others have died to find out. This is my first time on a boat. I'm taking my family to the new world where they will be safe. For some reason the new world is in the center of the Bermuda Triangle and that's where I'm headed before this world self destructs.

"H.O.U.S.E hack into the face book network and upload the selected files to all and every one of its members."

"Yes sir."

"After my family is safe I'm going after the agency. I feel like people should know what they've done and still are doing. I intend to find out who's over the whole operation . . .

Alday!

Made in the USA
Columbia, SC
26 May 2025

58448888R00045